Production and copyright © 2001 Rainbow Grafics Intl-Baronian Books,
63 rue Charles Legrelle, Brussels, Belgium.
English text copyright © 2001 Chronicle Books.

Book design by Jessica Dacher.
Typeset in Weiss.
Printed in Belgium.
ISBN 0-8118-3319-4

Library of Congress Cataloging-in-Publication Data available.

Distributed in Canada by Raincoast Books
9050 Shaughnessy Street, Vancouver, British Columbia V6P 6E5

10 9 8 7 6 5 4 3 2 1

Chronicle Books LLC
85 Second Street, San Francisco, California 94105

www.chroniclebooks.com/Kids

Will You Still Love Me?

*

by Jean-Baptiste Baronian
illustrated by Noris Kern

chronicle books · san francisco

Polo felt very sad.

Lately his mommy and daddy had been too busy to play with him.

It seemed they didn't love him anymore.

Polo wondered why.

So Polo set out to see if his friends could help him.

He found Walter the caribou, Jessie the
wolf, Felix the seal and Pinpin the penguin,
all fishing together.

Walter turned to Polo. "Polo, you look worried," he said.

Quietly Polo asked, "Do any of you know why my mommy and daddy don't love me anymore?"

"Maybe you've been naughty," said Pinpin.

"I can't remember having been naughty,"
Polo answered.

"What else could it be?" asked Felix.

Before Polo could answer, Pinpin's little brothers and sisters came rushing up.

"See you later, my mommy is waiting for us," said Pinpin.

"Mine too," said Felix. "Time to go."

Polo waved good-bye to his friends. Then he asked Jessie, "Do you know why my mommy and daddy don't love me anymore?"

"Maybe they still do," suggested Jessie. "Why don't you ask them?"

Polo thought about what his friend had
said, and then he headed home.

There he saw his parents snuggled close together. "What else could it be?" he wondered.

Polo looked closely at his mother. She looked different. Her tummy was big.

Then Polo heard his mother's voice.

"Polo, my sweet, what's wrong?"

"Mommy, why is your tummy so big?" Polo asked.

"That's where our new baby is growing," Polo's mother said. "Come here, close to me, and listen to the baby's little heartbeat. You're going to be a big brother soon."

Polo snuggled up against his mother. "A baby," he whispered. Then he looked at his mother. "Does that mean you and Daddy won't love me anymore?"

Polo's mother gave him a big hug. "Polo," she whispered back. "A mommy's heart is as big as the sea. And a daddy's heart is as big as the sky. I will always love you. Even when you are a big brother, you'll still be my little one. And I'll love both you and our new baby with all my heart."